THE COUCH POTATO

To Joel, Meiko, and Maia
—J.J.

For Anders
—P.O.

ISBN 978-1-338-83147-4

12 11 10 9 8 7 6 5 4 3 2 1   22 23 24 25 26 27

Printed in the U.S.A.   40

This edition first printing, January 2022

The artist used scanned watercolor textures and digital paint to create the illustrations for this book.

Typography by Jeanne L. Hogle

THE COUCH POTATO

WRITTEN BY **JORY JOHN**
ILLUSTRATED BY **PETE OSWALD**

I am a potato.

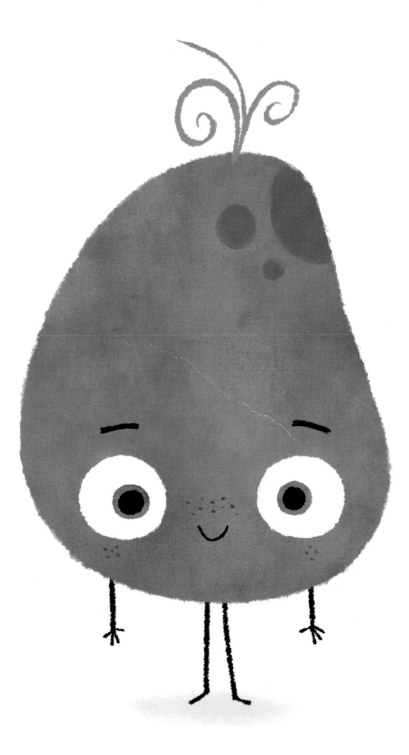

Not a small potato
like my brother.

Not a sweet potato
like my mother.

Not a mashed potato
like my uncle Stu.

I am a *couch* potato. Oh yeah, it's true! My favorite place to slouch is on the couch.
 I spend all my free time sitting in this exact spot.

Why would I ever leave this comfy, cozy couch?
It's got everything a potato could need....

See? I have this.

And this.

And this.

And one of these.

And those.

And this.

And that.

And these.

Oh, and *this*! Check it out. This button activates a gadget that fetches me snacks whenever I want.

Bam! Impressed? And I don't have to move an *inch*. *Much* easier than going to the kitchen.

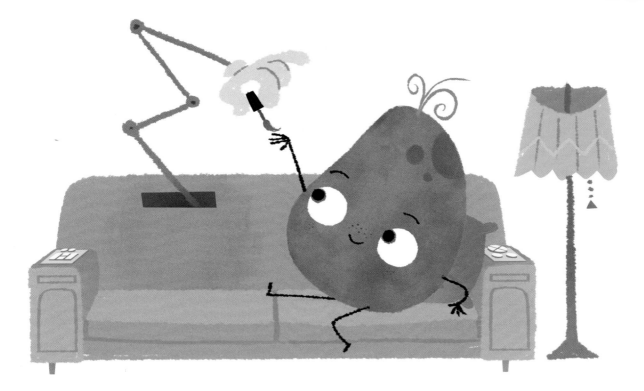

If the most *important* thing in life is to be comfortable at all times, then I think I've got it all figured out.

But wait, there's *more*!

I haven't revealed the absolute best part about my whole setup.

It's everything you see in front of me. Have a look around! Take it all in! Pretty spectacular, right?

Yes, it's a sea of shimmering screens, from wall to shining wall. What joy! What bliss!

These screens feature my favorite shows.

This screen has all my unanswered messages.

These screens are where I play video games.

And *this* screen is a livestream of my friend, my best spud for life!

This is how my pals and I spend quality time together. It's *much* easier than trying to meet up somewhere, like folks did in the old days. *That's* for sure.

"Hey, spuddy."

"Hey, pal-tato."

Yes, from this very couch, I can control everything in my life, all the time, with just a few taps and a couple clicks. Not bad, eh?

"AHHHHHHHHHHHHH."

Yessirree, this is the life.

At least, that's what I thought . . .
until the other day.

Something strange happened.
There was a knock at the door.
It was a delivery.

WHOOSH!

FRONT DOOR CAM

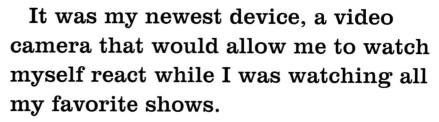

It was my newest device, a video camera that would allow me to watch myself react while I was watching all my favorite shows.

All I had to do was plug it in, and my room—nay, my kingdom!—would be complete. But suddenly . . .

PEW-WWWWWWWWW

Everything went dark!

"Look out!

Coming through!

Whoops! Oof!

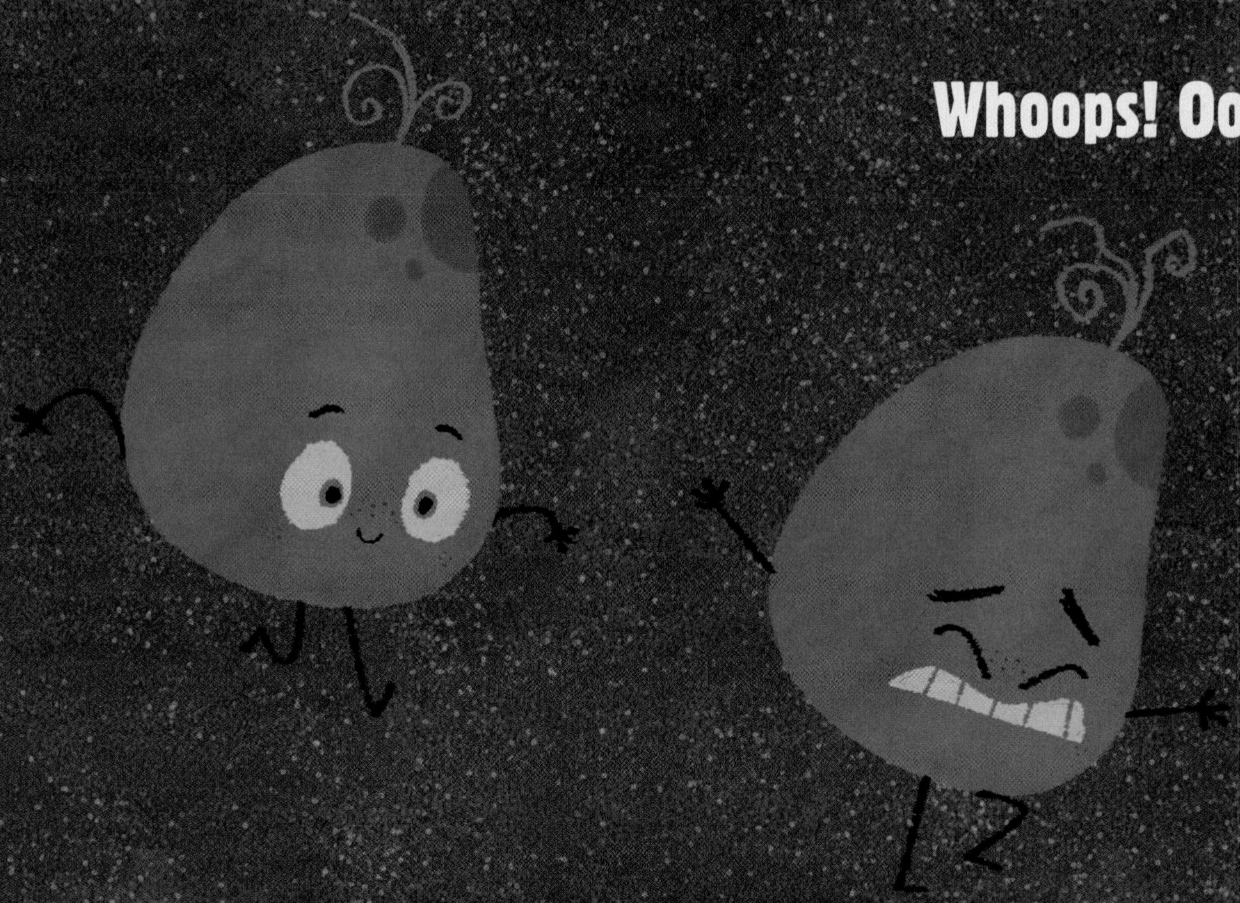

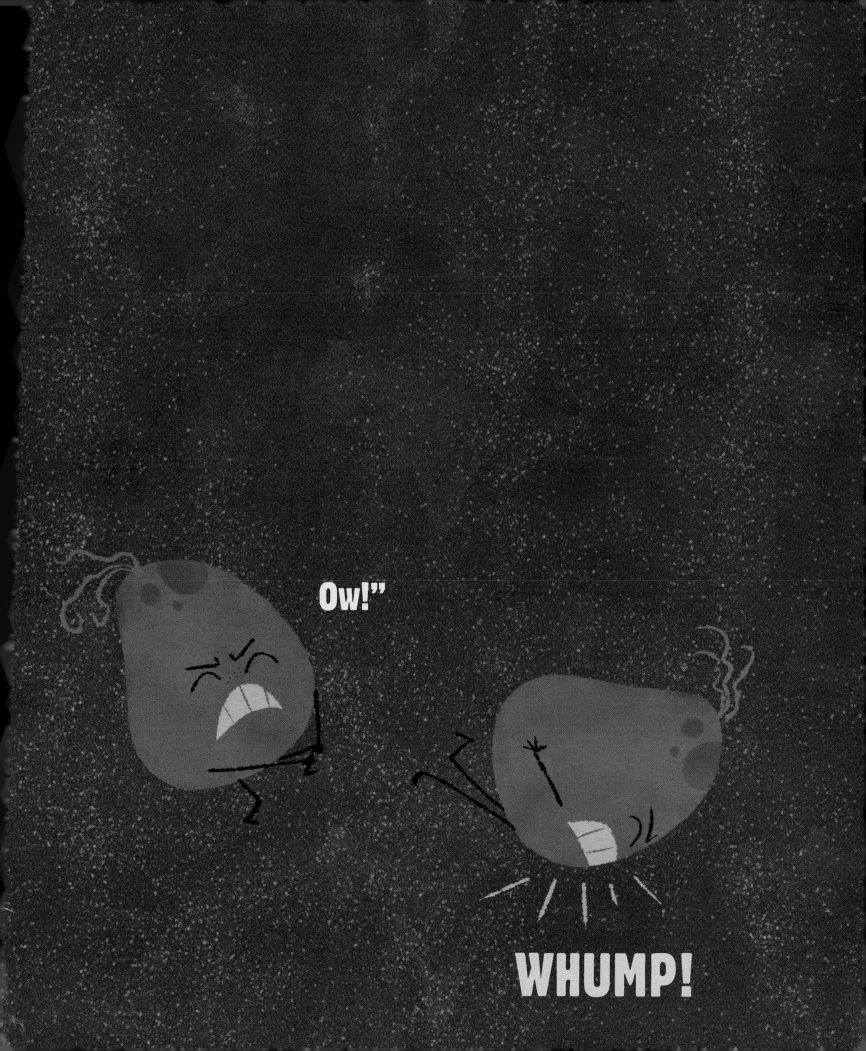

I made it to the window.
I pulled back the curtains.

The sun seemed brighter
than I remembered.

There was nothing better to do, so I decided to take
my dog, Tater, for a walk . . .

outside.

It had been a while.

Everything was so vivid, like a high-resolution 156-inch curved screen, but even *more* realistic.

Something smelled . . . fresh. After a few moments, I realized that it was the air.

I heard a noise. Some chirps. A ringtone, perhaps? But no. I looked up to see some birds.

I wandered down the street, from block to block, and across the neighborhood.

Eventually, I found a park with a
hill. There was a massive tree on top.
   It looked like a desktop
background . . . only it was *real*.

"Neat."

I leaned against the tree.
   It wasn't as comfortable as my
couch. Not even close.
   But after a while, it wasn't so bad.

"AHHHHHHH."

Any worries about the power outage and what I might be missing drifted away. I wasn't thinking about my favorite shows, or my unanswered messages, or anything else, really.

I noticed the stillness. The view. The sky. The clouds. The sunset. And those colors! My goodness.

It took a while, because there was no fast-forward option, but eventually the sun sank below the horizon.

By the time I got home,
the power was back on.
I sat on the couch.

I hit the button to
brush my teeth.

I pulled the lever to
change into my pajamas.

I turned the knob to watch a bedtime story.

I wondered how much of my life had been spent in that very spot.

It was then and there that I made the decision to peel myself off the couch a bit more often. Maybe every day, even.

And so that's what I've done.

I've started hanging out with my friends—my best spuddies!—outside.

We've started biking.

And hiking.

And swimming.

And hiding.

And seeking.

Sometimes we have snacks and play board games.
Sometimes we talk all day.
    We might watch the clouds. There's no big plan.
We just see what happens.

It makes me wonder . . . what if I don't always need to be totally comfortable? What if I'm happier when I have a better balance between my gadgets and the world outside?

Because it turns out that I'm more than just a couch potato.

I'm an amusing potato.

I'm a smart potato.

I'm a kind potato.

I'm an entertaining potato.

And I'm a *sit-on-a-hill-and-watch-the-sunset* potato.

Yes, there's a great big world out there . . .
and I want to be a part of it. In person.

But don't get me wrong. At the end of a long day—
after I've run and played and talked and laughed with
my friends . . .

I *still* think it's awfully nice to slouch on the couch.

JORY JOHN and **PETE OSWALD**
are the #1 *New York Times* bestselling creators
of *The Bad Seed*, *The Good Egg*, *The Cool
Bean*, and other books in their internationally
acclaimed series. Jory and Pete also
collaborated on the recent picture book *That's
What Dinosaurs Do* and the *New York Times*
bestselling *The Good Egg Presents: The Great
Eggscape!* Jory writes at home in Oregon and
Pete illustrates in his California studio.